THE FRIENDSHIP HOTLINE

Friends: How to Make 'Em, How to Keep 'Em!

Written by Nancy Krulik
Illustrated by Jon Nez
Foreword by Lois Berkowitz, PsyD.

PRICE STERN SLOAN

For Suzanne and Pat, who are like
the sisters I never had—N.E.K.

For Ann, Arthur, and Evan—J.N.

This book is not meant to replace advice from a psychologist or physician. Responsibility for adverse effects or unforeseen consequences resulting from the use of the information contained in this book is expressly disclaimed by the publishers and the author.

Text copyright © 1999 by Nancy Krulik. Illustrations copyright © 1999 by John Nez. All rights reserved. Published by Price Stern Sloan, a division of Penguin Putnam Books for Young Readers, New York. Printed in the United States of America. Published simultaneously in Canada. No part of this publication may be reproduced, stored in any retrieval system, or transmitted, in any form or by any means, electronic, mechanical, photocopying, recording or otherwise, without the prior written permission of the publisher.

Library of Congress Cataloging-in-Publication data is available.

ISBN 0-8431-7557-5   A B C D E F G H I J

Plugged in ™ is a trademark of Price Stern Sloan, Inc.
PSS! is a registered trademark of Penguin Putnam, Inc.

Table of Contents

Foreword
by Dr. Lois Berkowitz, PsyD.

The middle school and high school years pose many challenges. We worry about grades, about having more freedom, about how our bodies are changing, about dating, and about being liked. As we get further into our teens, being liked can get higher and higher on our list of priorities. That's a normal part of growing up and moving toward adulthood. What our parents believe still matters, but their opinions often get placed on the back burner in relation to what our friends think about us. Eventually, as we continue to mature, a balance will be struck in which others' thoughts and feelings matter, but we have a clearer idea of our own thoughts and feelings about important issues. We will take all of the rights and wrongs that

our parents taught us, as well as all that we have learned in our relationships with friends, and develop what is called a *sense of self*.

All human beings have needs for food, water, and shelter in order to survive. The idea that friendship is also needed for survival often gets dismissed. True, we can live without friendships, but an important building block to our sense of self will be missing. Humans aren't the only ones who depend on friendships to mature and grow—many animal species, such as elephants and gorillas, live in groups. When taken out of those groups, some of the animals have been known to literally die from loneliness. While that is not quite the case with human beings, everyone knows that loneliness is not a pleasant feeling.

Having friendships teaches us so much about sharing, cooperation, how to resolve conflicts, how to handle

intimacy, and just how to talk to people. We need these skills in order to go out into the world as adults and get jobs, find places to live, deal with coworkers, and find mates. But most importantly, friendships help us to feel good about ourselves by providing us with the feedback from another person that no matter what we do, that person will be there for us.

Certainly it is not okay to feel that the only way to like ourselves is to make sure that we are always liked by others. That can be a scary and insecure place to be. We don't want to have such low self-esteem that the only way we can feel good about ourselves is if others feel good about us. What happens then is that we are constantly trying to figure out what we need to do and say to people so as not to make them disapproving or critical of us. It takes a lot of energy to function that way, and no one will be successful one hundred percent of the time. Sooner or later we are bound to do or say something that our friends will not like. But it is important to make sure that our friends' disapproval does not lessen our sense of self.

Studies show that people with low self-esteem can become increasingly isolated—probably because it is too hard to try and anticipate what someone else wants to hear all of the time. In some cases, receiving negative feedback from another person can be so painful that a person just doesn't want to risk another friendship. This is an extreme situation, and one in which there might be problems in the person's life besides not having friends. In cases where not having friends is just one of several problems, such as feeling sad all of the time, having little or no appetite, having trouble sleeping, having difficulty concentrating, and generally feeling irritable, it may be time to talk to an adult you trust, or to seek counseling.

What this all comes back to is liking ourselves. Liking ourselves doesn't mean that we don't have areas we would like to improve upon. What having self-esteem means is that we can look in the mirror and see the same person with the same qualities regardless of the situation. The teen years are the time to solidify those qualities.

Our friendships are where we test out what we really think about everything from fashion and music to bigger issues like religion and right and wrong. That's why friendship and self-esteem are forever linked together. We need good self-esteem in order to form lasting friendships, and we need to have those friendships in order to continue to build a strong sense of self-esteem.

What Is a Friend, Anyway?

friend (noun): *One attached to another by affection or esteem.*

That's the dictionary definition of a friend. But those eight words really don't say it all, do they? The fact is, it's actually pretty hard to come up with one good definition for the word *friend.* Maybe that's because like people, there are no two friendships that are exactly alike.

But there are some characteristics that all good friends have in common. For instance, a friend is a person who knows when to talk, and when to listen. And not just when to listen, but how to hear what's really being said. A friend is a person who knows without being told when you need a pat on the back, or a shoulder to cry on. A friend is someone who laughs at your jokes, but never laughs behind your back.

A friend will be the person in the stands cheering the loudest when you run that big race. She'll always be there at the finish line with a hug—whether you win or lose.

A friend is someone you can share your dreams and hopes with. You can also talk to her about all the every-day boring details of your life. More importantly, a friend is a person with whom you can totally be yourself. You don't have to show off, or brag to a friend. She loves you just the way you are.

Wow! That's some job description. Obviously being a good friend is a lot of hard work. And it takes a great deal of time—something you may not have a lot of, considering how much homework you have, not to mention your after-school clubs, Saturday soccer league games, and baby-sitting responsibilities. But being a good friend is really worth the time and effort! When you think about it, being a friend is one of those rare opportunities in which you get back as much as you give. The more time and effort you put into a friendship, the stronger it becomes.

Friendship makes people brave. Just knowing that there is someone out there who really believes in you and who is guaranteed to be there to pick up the pieces if you fall, can be a very powerful force. It gives you the confidence to strive for things you never dreamed were possible. And being aware that someone else is counting on you for the exact same support will give you a sense of responsibility that you are certain to carry with you into every area of your life. Friendships help us grow as people. And that's what life is all about.

When you are a baby, the major influence in your life is your family. Those are the people you hang around with—and you don't get much choice in the matter. But as you get older and go to school, you develop a life outside of your home. That's when you start making friends—choosing the people you want to be influenced by, and upon whom you will have an influence. Some people even believe that when you're a teenager, your friends have more of an influence on your day-to-day life than your parents do! That's why it is so important to find friends who will allow you to stay true to yourself, and not try to pressure you to do things just to be part of the crowd.

This book is a salute to friendships. It's about the joys and hardships we go through when we find ourselves in the midst of one of those remarkable relationships. But remember: Relationships are not an exact science. In chemistry when you mix two parts hydrogen to one part oxygen, you know you'll get water. But unlike a chemistry experiment, you can't just follow the instructions in this book and be sure that the results will turn out the same time and again. What works for one set of friends will be absolutely useless for another. So instead of thinking of this book as a textbook about friendships, think of it as a springboard. Take the ideas within these pages and make them work for you.

What will you find inside this book? You name it—we've got it! You'll find tips on how to gain the confidence you need to go out there and meet people—in your home-town or across the world. You'll discover foolproof ways to steer clear of the traps that can split up a friendship, like cliques and rumors. You'll learn how to handle things if your best friend just happens to be a guy. There are even suggestions for ways you and your friends can disagree—without fighting. Basically, you'll discover that being a friend just means being yourself—and allowing your friends to do the same thing.

Chapter One

Loving the Friend
in the Mirror

Take a look in the mirror. Go ahead. Take a long, hard look. Who do you see there? A very good friend? Or an enemy who is making you miserable?

It's easy to notice all your faults when you look in the mirror—your hair is too curly, or your nose is too crooked, or your belly is just a little too round. It isn't

always as easy to notice the good things about yourself. But that's exactly what you have to do if you want to have long-lasting friendships.

It may not seem as though liking yourself will affect your relationships, but it really does. People usually treat others the same way they treat themselves. If you are critical of yourself, you are bound to be critical of other people. And that definitely won't score you any points in the friendship department.

Here's another surprise—other people tend to treat you the way you treat yourself. Everything you do sends out messages about the way you feel about yourself. Do you stand up straight and proud, or do you hunch over, trying to hide in the crowd? Do you smile brightly and with confidence, or do you frown a lot, always looking as though you have a rain cloud over your head? Your facial expressions, body language, and way of talking tells people exactly how you feel about yourself. If you enjoy your own company, it shows, and other people will want to enjoy your company as well. If you like yourself you will be more easygoing in social situations. And you will be less afraid of new challenges and experiences.

When you have confidence and self-esteem, you

open up your ability to love other people, and to have them love you. And that's really what friendship is all about. Everybody needs unconditional love. Why not give some to yourself?!

I like me! I really like me!

Okay, let's admit it. All this talk about liking yourself is definitely easier said than done. Society doesn't exactly bolster our self-esteem. Instead, it gives us impossible goals to live up to. Every magazine ad screams out that you practically have to be a model who looks like Barbie to make it in this world. But here's something to remember—Barbie is a plastic doll. And models have hairdressers, makeup artists, and (most importantly!) photographers who can airbrush all of their imperfections right out of a picture.

Have you ever said things like, "If only I were popular, I would feel better about myself," or "None of the boys in my class think I'm cute—I must not be too attractive"? If you have, wipe those thoughts right out of your head.

Self-confidence is not a mathematical equation that equals the sum of how you look plus how others feel about you. Self-confidence comes solely from within you. If you are searching for someone on the outside to make you feel good about yourself, it will never happen. The only person who can make you love yourself is you. You have to tell yourself that you are worth getting to know. That's what you'd tell a good friend, isn't it? So, be a good friend to yourself!

One way to start liking yourself is to say an affirmation every day. An affirmation is a positive statement about yourself. When you first start saying your daily affirmation, you may not truly believe what you are saying. But after days and days of repeating the same message to yourself, you will reprogram your brain to believe in what you are saying. By saying an affirmation over and over, you will change your life.

Don't believe it? Try this little test. Study your face in the mirror as you repeat this sentence over and over: "I like myself. I really like myself."

Did you notice something about your mouth? You smiled while you said the affirmation, didn't you? It's almost impossible to frown when you say, "I like myself." That's because your brain tells your body that this is a positive thought. And your body reacts to positivity with a smile.

Say "I like myself" often enough, and you'll start to believe it. But have patience. It might take you a while. Change is hard, and slow in coming. After all, people don't start out life with low self-esteem—it takes years to develop. High self-esteem can come more quickly, but it takes time, too. So don't give up.

Before you choose an affirmation for yourself, think about what it is you would most like to achieve. (Remember, liking yourself for who you are doesn't mean you can't change or improve things. You should always set goals for yourself. Your new-found confidence will help you reach your goals.)

Here's a list of affirmations that many people use every day. See if one fits you.

I like myself.
Life keeps getting better and better.
I deserve the best.
I'm a total winner!
There are no limits to what I can do.
I deserve success.
I am an attractive human being.
I am a really nice person.
I can say no—and feel good about it.
People will love me for who I am.
I can reach my potential.
I wasn't put on earth to fulfill the
 expectations of others.

I am the center of my universe.
My future is bright.
I have total confidence in myself.

Those affirmations are just a starting point. You can come up with some of your own, too. Here are a few pointers for creating an affirmation:

1. **Keep your affirmation short.**
2. **Make sure your affirmation is positive. Say "I look and feel healthy," instead of "I'm not as heavy as I used to be."**
3. **An affirmation needs to be in the present tense. This is how you want to feel right now!**
4. **Say your affirmation when you feel relaxed.**
5. **It's best to say your affirmation when you are alone.**
6. **Repeat your affirmation twice. Make sure you leave enough time between statements to let the message sink in.**

Now you know the kinds of things you need to be saying to yourself every day. But there are also a few words you need to avoid, because they will only bring you down. Strike these words from your mental dictionary:

should have
can't
impossible
difficult
doubt
if only

"Don't I have to do a little more than talk to feel good about myself?"

As the saying goes, talk is cheap! Affirmations alone will not automatically bolster your self-esteem. You need to live your affirmations. You can start out by simply acting out your words. If you affirm that you are attractive, then you have to go out into the world the way an attractive person would. Deep down you may still feel as though you want to hide, but dress nicely, do up your hair, polish your nails, stand tall, flash a big smile, and speak with power in your voice. You will be the attractive, terrific person you acknowledged in your affirmation.

I feel good!

Raising your self-esteem and your confidence are not the only ways you can be your own best friend. Best friends take care of each other. So take care of yourself.

You can start by fixing your diet. Candies and sodas may give you a temporary lift when you feel low or tired, but that lift is usually followed by a pretty quick drop. To feel good all the time, you have to learn to eat right. Buy yourself a few books on nutrition and discover how healthy foods can make you feel good. When you feel healthy, you feel better about yourself.

And while you're on this health kick, get moving! Take up an exercise routine—it can be something as simple as taking a regular half-hour walk around the neighborhood every day, or riding your bike back and forth to school. Or you can go for something a little more structured, like signing up for a dance class at the Y or joining an after-school sports team. (FYI: Never begin any kind of exercise program without checking with your doctor first.)

It may be hard in the beginning to take the time to make exercise a regular part of your life. After all, there are always other responsibilities tugging at you. But you have a responsibility to yourself. So be sure to make the time. Remember, as the TV commercial says, "I'm worth it!"

Chapter Two

Finding Friendship

Now that you've learned to accept and love the friend you see every day in the mirror, it's time to venture into the outside world and find some new friends.

I already have enough friends.
I don't need any more.
I'm skipping to Chapter Three!

Wait! Don't turn that page. If that's what you're thinking, you couldn't be more wrong. You can have enough earrings. You can have enough CDs. You can even have enough shoes (although it might take you years to accumulate them!). But you can never have enough friends.

The great thing about friends is that each one is different. And each one holds a special place in your life.

Some friends are great when you want to play some one-on-one hoops in your driveway. Others are great to go shopping with. Still other friends are wonderful to study with—especially if they are patient enough to explain to you for the forty-sixth time how to find the circumference of a circle!

When you make a new friend you get the chance to share different experiences. You just may discover that while you've always had a lot of superficial relationships, you've never really experienced a deep bonding friendship that can change your life. You don't want to pass up an opportunity like that, do you? Read on! You won't be sorry. Promise!

You're constantly surrounded by people. So how come you feel so lonely?

It's one of the strangest phenomenons in human nature. People living in the most crowded cities claim to feel the most alone. It sounds strange. After all, cities are filled with thousands of people, all literally living on top of one another. You would think it would be impossible to feel alone there. But it's actually very easy to feel anonymous in a crowd. There's nowhere you can feel more lonely than in a place where you are surrounded by people who you don't know and who don't know you.

Now you may not live in a city, but it's possible that you are surrounded by people who don't know the real you—and who aren't really close to you either

Even though you may play soccer with a group of terrific kids, and there's that girl from your English class who hangs out with you at lunch, you can still feel lonely. Superficial relationships can fill up your time, but they can't fill the need we all have for one good friend whom we can depend on.

No doubt about it. Feeling lonely stinks! But being lonely is part of life. Everyone goes through it—from the most popular girl in your school, to mega-celebrities like Madonna and Brad Pitt. And knowing that even they have moments where they would trade all the glitz, glamour, and screaming fans for five minutes with a good friend, can somehow make you feel a little better about your situation.

Use the time when you feel lonely as an opportunity to grow. Think about what kind of person could fill that void in your life. Then go out and find yourself a new good friend—or maybe two!

Do you believe in friendship at first sight?

When it comes to making friends, luck can sometimes play a big part. Once in a very great while, your path may cross with someone who is meant to be your lifelong friend. Maybe she's got a laugh that is so infectious that one of her giggles can set everyone in the room roaring. Or, maybe she's got a certain sparkle in her eye that makes you feel instantly drawn to her. So you walk over and introduce yourself (you can do that, because you have confidence!). She smiles, and starts up a conversation. Suddenly, you feel like you've known each other forever.

Before long, you and your new friend are practically joined at the hip—shopping together, going to the movies, and pairing up for your science fair project. And deep down you both know that no matter where life takes you, the two of you will always be the best of friends.

Some friendships really do begin that way. But the truth is, most of them don't. And if you spend your whole life waiting for that feeling of instant closeness, you're going to miss out on some pretty terrific people.

Don't wait for the gift of friendship.

Friendship is a gift that people give one another. But if you wait around for it to show up wrapped in a pret-

ty box with a big red bow, you might be lonely for a very long time.

If you want to make new friends, sometimes you've got to make the first move. Start by thinking about the kinds of things you like to do. Are you an outdoors type who thinks hiking is as close to heaven as you can get? Or are you more the arts and crafts type whose favorite birthday gift would be a subscription to *Martha Stuart Living*? Do you dream of someday being a rock musician; or is ballet more your style? Whatever your idea of fun, guaranteed there are other kids your age who agree.

Once you know where your heart lies, follow it! Join the hiking club at school. Take a pottery class at the Y.

Sign up for the school band, or take an advanced dance class.

Clubs and classes are definitely a great way to meet new people. For starters, you know that you share an interest with everyone else there. And, classes and clubs are usually small groups. That means you'll get a chance to talk to everyone there.

If someone in your group seems kind of cool, strike up a conversation with her before or after class. That won't be as hard as you think—remember, you already have something in common. Talk about what your group or club is working on. If you guys seem to get along, suggest checking out a movie or going to the mall over the weekend.

Of course there is always the possibility that you won't seem to click with anybody in your new class or club. And that's okay, too, because you will still be doing something you love. Finish out the course, and then try a different one, filled with all new people.

Why can't we be friends?

Here's a not-so-terrific fact: Not every attempt at making friends is going to be a success. It takes two people to make chemistry happen. And if you are the only one who feels the chemistry, then you're going to get very little reaction from the other person.

Sometimes it's hard to tell whether a person is not interested in a new friendship or if she's just shy. One way to tell is if she seems more outgoing and friendly around other people than she is around you. If you call her and she says she's too busy to go to the movies, but you notice she always seems to have time to go bike riding with someone else, perhaps this friendship is just not meant to be.

There's only so much you can do when you are trying to develop a friendship with someone. You can call her, invite her to events, and even sit down beside her at lunch. But if after a while you discover that those phone calls only seem to be going in one direction and that she's always busy with something else when you ask her to go for a bike ride or to catch a movie, it may be time for you to take the hint.

Rejection is painful. But it isn't necessarily something you did or said, that caused her to decide not to become your friend. You may never find out what went wrong. So why stay up nights worrying about it? Accept her rejection as one of life's little mysteries, and be grateful for the friends you do have.

Make new friends, but keep the old. . . .

You may have been born in the very town you're living in now. Since you've spent your whole life there, you know just about everyone. That does make having friends a lot easier. After all, you've got a lot of history with kids you've shared a playpen with. But imagine how it would feel to be brand new in school. Everyone there knows one another. And you don't know anybody. Talk about scary!

If there's a new kid in your school, do your good deed for the day and volunteer to be her buddy for a week. You can show her around the school, help her find her classes, and introduce her to some of your friends. She'll appreciate the help, and you may discover that you and she have a lot in common.

Help Wanted:
New kid desires friendly face
to make her feel more at home.

If you're the new kid in town, you must be feeling really frightened right about now. All those strange faces and names to remember can seem overwhelming. But take a deep breath. Things will work out. After a few days, you'll begin to recognize kids from your classes as they walk through the halls. And that's the first step.

Look for the people who seem to have interests that are similar to yours. Maybe one girl has plastered the cover of her notebook with pictures of a group you really love. Go over and ask her if she'd like to come over one afternoon and listen to their latest CD on your new stereo system. Someone else might wear clothes you absolutely adore. Ask her if she can show you some of the really cool spots to shop. It can be uncomfortable at first, but keep your affirmations in mind—they will make it easier for you to go over and introduce yourself to new people. Before long, you will have gotten to know plenty of kids at your new school.

Of course, not all of the girls you meet will turn out to be good friends for you. Some may just turn out to be superficial buddies to chat with in class. Others may have interests that just don't jibe with yours. But the chances are good that several of the kids you meet will become your friends. And wherever you have friends, you will feel at home.

Chapter Three

Gaining the Courage to Say Hello

Alicia was extremely shy. The thought of meeting new people was paralyzing to her—in fact the only friends she had were those she had known since she was a baby.

Alicia's friends often invited her to come along with them to parties. Alicia usually begged off because she knew what would happen if she went. It was the same thing every time—Alicia stood in the corner by the food and watched everyone else have a good time. No one ever went over to talk to her, and Alicia wound up crying into her pillow at night.

Alicia's friend Lexi suggested that Alicia tell herself that she wasn't shy. She told Alicia that when she got to the party she should constantly say to herself, "I am not afraid. I am not afraid. I am not afraid."

And that's exactly what Alicia did. What do you think happened?

If you said you believed that Alicia had a wonderful time at the party that night, you would be totally incorrect. Surprise!

By completely denying that her feelings existed, Alicia put herself into a state of confusion. Her body tensed up and the look on her face let everyone at the party know that she was uncomfortable. And so, others left her alone.

By saying that she wasn't afraid, Alicia was lying to herself. And when you lie, your body knows it. Your heartbeat increases, and your blood pressure rises. Someone whose heart is beating too fast, definitely does not look relaxed and confident.

At first glance it might seem that Alicia was stating an affirmation by saying, "I am not afraid." But that's not an affirmation. First of all, affirmations aren't negative, remember? And more importantly affirmations are not lies. They're truths that you state over and over again. You really are a valuable person, and if you work hard enough, you can accomplish anything you put your mind to.

If you're like Alicia, and you feel like every new party is a danger zone to be avoided, there are some tricks you can try to feel more relaxed and more confident.

One way to let go of fear is to visualize it and let it go. Close your eyes and imagine your fear as a big black balloon hanging over your head. You hold the balloon by a string. Now let go of that string. In your mind, watch that big old balloon floating higher and higher toward the sky. It becomes smaller, and smaller until, finally, all of your fear has disappeared. Anytime that old shyness panic comes back, close your eyes and let it go again.

Visualization works really well when you combine it with other confidence-boosting techniques. While you are visualizing your fear disappearing, try repeating this affirmation: Strangers are friends to be. Strangers are friends to be. Keep saying this affirmation, and keep living as though you believe it.

Hopefully, when your next party invitation arrives, you'll be ready for it. But chances are, you'll still feel a few butterflies on the night of the big shindig. And that's okay! As you enter the party, allow yourself to admit that you're nervous. Accept it. Tell yourself, "I'm afraid, but I am stronger than my fears." Then try and recall how your body feels at its most confident state. Try to get your body to take on the look of a confident person. If you look confident and comfortable, people will start to come over and chat. Chat back. Before long, you'll be having a good time!

Chapter Four

Three Is Not a Crowd

Jamie and Katherine had been best friends since first grade. They practically grew up in each other's homes. They never hung out with anyone else. After a while, the other kids began to stay away, which never really bothered Jamie or Katherine because they always had each other.

Everything was going just fine until the summer before Jamie and Katherine entered eighth grade. That year Jamie's family decided to take an extended summer vacation at a house on the beach. Katherine's parents sent her to a sleepaway camp that lots of kids from her school were going to.

Jamie and Katherine sent letters back and forth every day for the first few weeks of the summer. But after a while, Jamie noticed that although she was still writing, she wasn't getting any letters back from Katherine.

Jamie came home in the fall, and called Katherine right away. She wanted to know if Katherine wanted to go to the mall with her. But Katherine was busy hanging out with a new friend whom she'd met at camp. Jamie asked her about going the next day, but Katherine made it clear that she and her new best friend were going to be spending all of their time together. Katherine would no longer have time for Jamie.

Jamie was devastated. Especially when she realized that she would be going back to school without having any friends at all.

Do you know any girls like Katherine and Jamie? You probably do. In every school, there's always a pair of best friends who are inseparable. And like Katherine and Jamie, any two friends who hang out exclusively are heading straight for disaster!

Having a best friend can be a wonderful thing. It's great to have a special someone to tell your secrets to, go places with, and share private jokes with. It's nice to know that there's someone out there who loves you for yourself and who doesn't judge you. But having a best friend shouldn't mean that you don't hang out with anybody else. When you do that, you walk straight into the same dangerous trap Jamie found herself in. Guaranteed, at least one of you (and probably both of you) are going to get hurt!

Luckily, it's easy to avoid the "three's a crowd" trap. All you and your best friend have to do is make sure you both spend lots of time with other people—together, and on your own.

One great way is to join a local sports team. On a team, members all work together for a common goal. That means that you and your best friend will get to work side by side with lots of other kids. And you really can't pair off into an exclusive group. You have to talk to other people when you are all on the same team.

Kids join teams for all different reasons. Some kids are really athletic, and they're looking for a way to use that talent. Some kids need the exercise, and they figure soccer or softball is a whole lot more fun than leg lifts and ab crunches. Still other kids join teams to make new friends. The best part about a team is that kids from all different backgrounds and cliques get to meet and work together. You get to make friends with people you might never have spoken to in a school setting. And there's an added bonus—playing sports is great for your body!

You and your best friend will probably make some new friends on the team. You, your best friend, and your new friends may all decide to hang out together, going to the mall, or having a victory picnic somewhere. But sometimes you and your best pal may decide to hang out separately with different teammates. And that's okay. In fact, it's probably good for you.

Oh no! My best friend has made some new friends. Our relationship is doomed!

It's easy to feel threatened when your best friend has made some new buddies. You start to feel like you are going to wind up having lunch all by yourself, and watching TV with your parents on Saturday night.

But it isn't necessarily going to be like that. Remember: One of the most basic rules of friendship is trust. You have to trust that your best friend still loves you, even though she's widened her horizons a bit. If you think about it, Katherine couldn't have been a true best friend to Jamie. A true best friend would never dump her pal for someone else. If Katherine were truly Jamie's best friend, she would have invited Jamie to come along and meet her friend from camp. There's no rule that says three girls can't be best friends! Maybe you can hang out with some of your friend's new pals, too.

The best thing to do when your best friend has made some new friends is to make some new friends of your own. Hanging out with other people doesn't mean you are being disloyal to your best friend. It just means that you enjoy other people's company as well. And when you make new friends you expand your horizons— which makes you grow as a person. And that can only benefit your relationship with your best friend.

Believe it or not, there is a downside to making new friends—it will cut into the time you and your best friend spend alone together. After all, there are only so many days in a week. Even so, you and your best friend should have plenty of time for each other. Be sure never to break plans with your best friend to do something with your new friends.

Another way to make sure you and your best friend remain as close as ever is to start keeping a "Best Friends' Diary." A Best Friends' Diary is a shared journal that you pass back and forth between each other. You can write anything you want in the diary—you can tell her about something that happened to you when she wasn't there, ask each other questions, glue in pictures of things you've done together, or write down things that have been bothering you. And you can feel assured that your secret feelings will stay secret, because nobody ever sees a Best Friends' Diary except for you and your best friend. The greatest part about a Best Friends' Diary is that years from now you two have a whole memory book that is just about your friendship.

To dump or not to dump?
That is the question.

Okay, here's the situation. Suppose your new friends don't like your best friend. They say she's a total nerd, and anyone who hangs around with her must be a nerd, too. It's either her or them!

Deep down, when you get in this situation, you know what the right thing to do is. You should dump those new friends, and stick with your best friend. She's always been there for you, and you should be there for her.

But that's easier said than done, isn't it? Peer pressure is a tough thing to beat. After all, you like your new friends. And they are part of a very big, cool crowd. What if they decide to make you a social outcast, because you chose to stick by your best friend?

You might be tempted to drop your best friend so your new friends will still like you.

If this thought has crossed your mind, don't feel guilty. You are not the first kid to be put into this position, and you won't be the last. But you do have a big decision to make...maybe!

That's right, *maybe*. There is a way that you may be able to keep your new friends while still staying loyal to your best buddy. Chances are your new friends don't really know your best friend. Kids only pin labels on people they don't know very well. When people actually meet someone and get to talking with her, they automatically begin to see her for who she is, not as part of some group.

If you think that your new friends might like your best friend once they get to know her, give it a try. Start by arranging for you, your best friend, and one of your new chums to get together. Plan to meet at a neutral place—maybe take in a movie and then go for a soda at the mall. The three of you will get a chance to talk. Since there isn't a whole crowd around, your new

friend is less likely to be swayed by peer pressure into automatically dismissing your best buddy. It just may turn out that those two will become friendly as well, making your life a whole lot easier. But if that doesn't work, and you continue to be pressured by your new friends to give your best pal the old heave-ho, you really have no choice but to stick by your best friend. Try saying an affirmation especially designed to pull you through a problem like this: "I can say no and feel good about it!".

As painful as it may seem at first, you will eventually be glad you did the right thing. Kids who expect you to do whatever they ask just so you can hang out with them, aren't really friends at all. And by asking you to give up someone you really care about they are demonstrating that they don't understand the importance of loyalty in a relationship. Think about it. Even if you do the unthinkable, and leave your best friend behind, there's no guarantee that your new friendships will last. The next person they dump could be you. And then where would you be?

Chapter Five

Meet My Best Friend...John!

Girl and Guy:
Best friends 4Ever!

*D*awson's Creek's Dawson and Joey. *Clueless's* Cher and Josh. *When Harry Met Sally's* Harry and Sally. Boy, Hollywood would sure like us to believe that guys and girls can never have friendships unless

there's romance involved. We've all seen the shows—there's a guy and a girl, best buddies, each searching for their ultimate soul mate. It may take them months, or even years, but eventually they discover that the person they were looking for was always there, right beside them. And suddenly, best friends become so much more. According to Hollywood, guys and girls can't be friends, unless they are romantically involved.

Well, here's a big message to all those Hollywood producers out there—you're wrong! Girls and guys can be friends. Really and truly.

Having a guy for a best friend may not be the typical way to go, but when you find someone whom you can trust, talk to, be there for, and have fun with, why argue about the person's sex? Just thank your lucky stars you've found a good friend.

Of course, the rules do have to change somewhat when a guy is your best friend. Joey and Dawson not withstanding, sleepovers are a definite no-no when your best friend is a guy. And clothes shopping in the mall is probably not high on your list of activities to share with your best buddy. (Chances are if your best friend is a guy, a marathon shopping spree is probably not your idea of how to spend a Saturday, anyway.)

Having a guy for a best friend does have some definite advantages. For starters, you can go to school dances together—provided neither of you is interested in asking someone else. At least you are guaranteed that you will have a great time with the person you are there with—best friends don't have to waste time trying to impress one another or playing all those silly dating head games.

Another big benefit to having a best friend who is a guy is that you don't have to search very far to get a male perspective on things. And that's good, because a lot of what makes girls shy in school is the fear of what the boys will think. But if your best friend is a guy, and he likes you just the way you are, then it stands to reason that other guys will feel the same way.

Which leads us to one of the major pitfalls in a friendship between a boy and a girl.

My best friend's a guy and I can't get a date. How ironic is that?!

Let's face it. The first thing other guys may think when they see a girl and a guy together is that they are going out. If you have a guy for a best friend, you know that's not necessarily the case. But how do you let other guys know you're available?

One way is simply to take the first step when you find a guy you are interested in, in a romantic sort of way. You can even ask him out. (Reread Chapter One if you need a little self-esteem boost before you ask him.) The chances are good that when you do, the guy is going to say something like, "But what about John?" (or Sam or Jamal or Paolo or whatever your best friend's name is). That's when you explain that you and he are not going out. You're best friends.

Some guys can accept that. Some guys can't. But if the guy you've chosen doesn't like the idea of his girlfriend having a guy for a best friend, then you know he's not the right guy for you.

If you're not the kind of girl who can go right up to a guy and ask him out, there is something else you and your best friend can do to help the situation. Have a talk with your best buddy and explain the situation to him. Because best friends can talk about anything, he's sure to understand. In fact, he may be having similar problems attracting girls who don't want to go out with him out of loyalty to you! You two may have to make a pact to spend more time hanging out in large groups for a while—that way you can still be together and with other people. Being part of a crowd will give your relationship less of a romantic look to outsiders.

Eventually the other kids in your group will get to know you both well enough to understand your relationship. But you shouldn't give up those long talks or study sessions—don't let anyone take away the most important aspects of your friendship. Boyfriends come and go, but a best friend is a lifetime investment!

Uh-oh!
I've got a crush on my best friend!

Okay, so Hollywood isn't always wrong. Sometimes romantic relationships do blossom out of friendships. But this is a bridge you'd better be very careful about crossing.

Before you burst out and kiss your best friend, take a long hard look at your feelings. Are you sure you feel

of life is that romantic relationships—especially those in middle school and high school—often come to an end. And although you both may feel that your friendship is strong enough to withstand that, there is that possibility that the end of the romance will be the end of your best friend status. You may remain friends, but that ability to listen without judging or getting jealous might no longer be possible after a romantic relationship—especially if one of you decides to break off the romance before the other.

No one can tell you how to play this one. It's up to you to weigh the pros and cons and decide what to do. Good luck!

Chapter Six

Learning to Listen

The greatest gift one friend can give another can't be wrapped in a box, or sent special delivery with a singing telegram. It can't be bought in a store, or ordered over the Internet. That's because the greatest gift you can give someone is the attention and respect it takes to listen to her when she needs to be heard.

Listening is hard work. It means putting your own opinions aside and opening your mind to your friend's point of view. That may seem like a simple thing to do, but it's not. Still, when you think about the happiness it will bring to your friend, you realize that learning to actively listen is worth the effort.

Hey! Stop butting in on my stories!

Interrupting is one of the most common problems people have when they are trying to learn how to listen. Many people are simply natural-born talkers. They want to make themselves heard. They want their opinions to be taken seriously and understood. But when someone else comes to you with a problem, it is more important to be understanding than to be understood.

If you interrupt someone, it means you've been spending the conversation thinking about what you are going to say next, instead of waiting to hear what your friend is trying to say. That's a basic lack of respect. Besides, if you're so busy thinking about what you're going to say next, you may miss an important piece of the puzzle—the piece that just may help your friend solve her problem.

Luckily, you can train yourself to stop interrupting. Simply wait until your friend is finished speaking. Then take a slow breath before you reply. Remind yourself that a conversation between friends is not the Indy 500. You don't win if you get the most words in at the fastest speed.

Friendship is not a test—
no corrections are needed.

What's wrong with this picture? Mary tells her friend Sue that she feels as though her friends are too busy with their after-school activities to want to hang out with her anymore. She believes they are dumping her. Sue laughs and tells Mary to get a grip. Mary's feelings are totally wrong. She's being too paranoid. Besides, if she wants to keep her friends, she'd better stop expecting them to be there for her 24/7.

Here's a major point for everyone to remember. Feelings are never wrong. What somebody feels is always valid, even if somebody has misunderstood the circumstances leading up to those feelings.

There's another problem here as well. Sue is correcting Mary, and telling her how to behave if she wants to

keep her friends. That sets up a very uncomfortable imbalance in the friendship. When you correct someone, you are making a big assumption. You're saying that you know more than the other person does. That makes one friend the teacher and the other friend the student. When you think of it that way it sounds pretty arrogant, doesn't it?

There are lots of problems with correcting a friend when she comes to you with her troubles. For starters, you may be missing the point of why she turned to you in the first place. Your friend may not have wanted to know what you think. She may have come to you because she knows you will always be there for her and never judge her, and she just wanted someone to listen.

Another problem with correcting your friend is that your criticism won't help her in any way. People rarely learn anything from even the most lovingly offered constructive criticism. (When's the last time you said to your great-aunt, "Thank you for telling me to stand up straighter and pull my hair off my face"?) Too much criticism could also mean the end to your friendship. After a while, your friend is likely to become defensive and you two might start having an argument. Even worse, if you are too critical, your friend may stop talking to you about her problems because she feels afraid or ashamed of seeming silly or wrong. Which of course is not at all what you had in mind. So here's a good rule of thumb: When it comes to friendship, you don't always have to be right. But you do always have to show you care. So keep listening, and leave the correcting to your teachers.

FYI: Correcting someone is not the same as making a suggestion as to how your friend can fix a problem. Gentle, loving advice can be very helpful to someone who really needs to be pointed in the right direction before she can solve her own problem.

It's hard to know when a friend wants advice and

when she just wants you to listen. So here's a general rule of thumb to follow: The time to give advice is after you've been asked for it. When one friend asks another for advice, it means that she is willing and able to listen to the suggestion, and really hear what is being said. If you try giving advice before you are asked for it, your words will almost certainly come up against deaf ears and a closed mind.

Remember, you can't give good advice if you haven't heard the whole problem. So sit back and really listen. Then, hopefully, you and your friend will be able to work out the problem, together.

Chapter Seven

Popping the Popularity Myth

Did you know:

*Country music sensation Terri Clark was considered "weird" by the kids in her Canadian high school because she wore cowboy boots and Wrangler jeans to school every day?

*Number-one hit sensation Mariah Carey was jokingly voted "Miss Mod" by her graduating class because of the strange (yet stylish) outfits she put together?

*Grammy-grabbing singer Paula Cole couldn't get a date to her senior prom?

It's true. Not one of these entertainers were considered popular when they were growing up. But look at them now. Terri's weird clothing now earns her millions of dollars a year as a spokesperson for Wrangler. Mariah has had more number ones than any other female recording artist. And Paula Cole has recorded the theme song for the oh-so-popular TV show *Dawson's Creek*!

It just goes to show that you don't have to be popular as a kid to be successful as an adult. In fact, the opposite can be true. Studies show that if life comes too easily for you when you are in school, you never develop the ability to roll with the punches; to cope with the hard times. And that can hurt you later in life. But people who have had to face problems when they were kids, develop the stamina and coping strategies necessary to become successful, happy adults.

Nice to know, isn't it?

What labels do you wear?

Here's an assignment. Look around at the kids in the hallways of your school. Can you tell what group each of those kids is in based on what he or she is wearing or what classes he or she is taking?

What names did you come up with? The cool, popular kids? The jocks? The nerds? The artists? After you've identified all of the groups in your school, make a promise never to think of people in that way again. When it comes to people, labels don't define you, they confine you!

People are naturally drawn to others who have the same interests as they do. We like to go to rock concerts with people who like the same music, or play a game of tennis with someone else who's really good at rallying the ball. But when you only hang out with people who seem to be just like you, you are limiting yourself. There may be a lot of people out there whom you might find very interesting—even if they would rather spend their Saturdays at the planetarium than at the mall.

When you think about it, the criteria people use to place others into groups don't make much sense. A lot of the time what group you get thrown into is based on the clothing or amount of makeup you wear, the music you listen to, the classes you take, and even things that have nothing to do with you—like how much money

Artist   Jock   Stuck-Up

your parents make, or where your family spends their vacation.

Those things really shouldn't matter. Wearing clothes from the GAP doesn't make you any different than someone who buys at vintage stores, does it? And what is it about Air Jordans that can make a person cool? It's not like they are Dorothy's ruby slippers, with enough magic power to take you from Oz to Kansas just by tapping your heels! And yet every day, kids spend thousands and thousands of dollars, trying to dress like a small group of people who may not be as happy on the inside as they appear on the outside.

Right now it might seem that what crowd you hang out with is extremely important to your identity. But that's not true. In fact, by the time you reach college,

Brainy   Nerd   Hippy

nobody is going to care whether you were a cheer-leader or in the chess club. All they'll care about is how smart, charming, and interesting you are. And by the time you get your first full-time job, the words nerd, jock, and popular will be almost completely gone from your vocabulary. So why not get a jump-start on adulthood and become friendly with the people you like, no matter what their label?

How popular are the popular kids?

Every school has its so-called popular crowd. You know, that small clique of kids who not only know what's in and what's out, but actually determine it. They're the ones who set the standards. The ones everyone else wants to hang with at lunch. They're kind of like celebrities—but on a much smaller scale.

But is that really popular? The dictionary defines *popular* as being, "of or relating to the general public; commonly liked or approved."

That's not what defines the popular kids in school. In fact, most of the kids in popular groups aren't commonly liked at all. And they are often pretty choosy as to whom they hang around with.

A teenager interviewed in *The New York Times Magazine* once declared that "the people in the popular group say there is no peer pressure. That's because they are at the top of the food chain."

But that teenager was wrong. People in the popular crowd can definitely fall victim to peer pressure. In fact, in some ways the pressure to stay on top is more stressful than just wanting to be more popular than you are.

The problem with being popular is that you have to work so hard at it. You have to be constantly in touch with what's new and cool—and you have to have it. But needing to be the first to buy new dresses or lipsticks that change color with your mood isn't the hard part of peer pressure. The problems come when the only way you can stay in the popular group is by doing things that you don't believe in, so that your "friends" will allow you to remain one of them.

It could start with something as simple as being told that what you love is totally uncool.

Melissa was a freshman cheerleader in a suburban high school. Melissa had a secret dream—she wanted to be an actress on the Broadway stage. She always loved performing—in fact, that was part of the reason she had joined cheerleading in the first place. It was like being on stage every week, dancing before a huge, enthusiastic crowd.

When it came time to audition for the school musical, Melissa spent hours at her piano, working on her audition song. But just before the auditions, some of the older cheerleaders pulled her aside and told her that if she wanted to hang out with the other cheerleaders, she would have to forget about being in the musical. Hanging out with the theater kids was totally uncool.

Melissa decided that there was plenty of time to be an actress, and she withdrew her name from the auditions. But she regretted it every time she would pass by the auditorium and see the cast rehearsing. The kids looked as though they were having so much fun. And they seemed free to experiment with their talents and try new ideas onstage. That was something the older cheerleaders discouraged in the freshmen. Melissa discovered too late that she should have followed her heart instead of caving in to the peer pressure of her fellow cheerleaders. She vowed that the following year she would try out for any play she wanted to.

Melissa had it easy. She was only pressured into withdrawing from a play. And she was able to correct her mistake the following year.

But not all peer pressure is so harmless. As you get older, you'll be faced with a lot of temptations. You'll hear people tell you that it's cool to shoplift, smoke cigarettes, drink alcohol, or do drugs. In your heart, you may feel that these things are not cool. In your mind, you may know that they can be harmful. But peer pressure is a tough thing to fight. We all have a desire to belong. But you shouldn't have to compromise your own beliefs or personal well-being in order to belong.

Saying "no" is tough. So prepare yourself for it by saying some simple affirmations.

It's okay for me to say no.
The only "shoulds" I listen to are my own.
I am a wonderful, worthy human being.
I determine my own self-worth.

The simple truth is that if someone is really your friend, they won't ask you to be someone you're not. They'll love and accept you for who you are.

What happens now?

There's no sense lying about it. When you refuse to go along with what the crowd is doing, you may lose some of your acquaintances. Notice the word *acquaintances*. You'll never lose real friends just because you don't do what they're doing. Real friends will respect the fact that you are sticking to your convictions. And as for those other people, think of it this way: As far as friends go, you can't lose what you never really had.

Although it might hurt to suddenly find yourself on the outs with people you trusted, try and see the positive in what has happened. First of all, you now know who your real friends are. And that lesson is worth more than anything. Secondly, you've broken free of the constraints of being in a crowd. You can hang out with everybody! That means more friends! More importantly, you've remained true to your beliefs. And as your own best friend, you really should expect nothing less of yourself.

Chapter Eight

How to Have
a Successful Argument

*Sometimes I can't believe the things
that come out of my best friend's mouth!*

Sooner or later, it's bound to happen. You and your friend are going to disagree. And not just slightly. You're going to think that her opinion is totally off the wall. And she's going to find it hard to believe that anyone in her right mind would think the way you do.

It takes two people to have a relationship. Each person brings her own likes and dislikes to the table. Because our personal histories influence the way we react to situations, you and your friends are going to feel differently about things from time to time. It's easy to let these differences pull you apart. It's far more difficult to try and work out your disputes. But hey, you've known from the beginning that nothing worth having comes easy. And friendship is definitely worth having.

There's no such thing as winning an argument. If you were to win, then your friend would have to lose. And making your friend feel as though she's lost is a hurtful thing to do. So keep in mind that when you argue, your goal is to come to some sort of compromise that makes you both happy. You really can accomplish that goal. If you follow these few rules, you and your friend should be able to talk things through, come to an agreement, and leave your argument behind you.

RULE 1
Separate the person from the action.

Have you ever said to anyone, "I am so angry with you!"? Sure you have. Who hasn't? But when you say that, you're not really telling the truth. What you mean to say is, "I am so angry with what you have done." Being able to separate what your friend has done from who she is will allow you to go on loving your friend, even when you don't necessarily agree with her actions. And because you love your friend, you'll be more eager to forgive her.

RULE 2
Stick to the topic.

If you're angry about something your friend has said or done, then discuss that. Don't let your mind wander back over every little thing that your friend has ever said or done that has annoyed you. Let's say you are angry because your best friend went with her cousin to see a movie that she promised she would see with you. It won't help matters to bring up that time in second grade when she shared her fruit roll-up with somebody else, even though you wanted it. Discussing all of that past history will only make both you and your friend more angry with each other.

RULE 3
Give yourself a time-out.

Remember when you were a little kid and you got so angry that you threw sand at the little boy who took your truck? What did your mother do? Most likely she gave you a time-out. The time-out wasn't a punishment, it was a chance for you to calm down.

When you say something cruel to a friend, there's no taking it back. Once the words are out of your mouth, they are written forever in the history of your friendship. Sure, you and your friend can make up, and maintain your relationship. But things will never be exactly the same again.

So when you feel so upset that you know you will not be able to control your temper, give yourself a short time-out. Go home, take a deep breath, and try to sort out your feelings. Write down the things you want to say. When you feel calm, cool, and collected, call your friend and suggest that you meet to talk things out.

RULE 4
Don't let it go on too long.

Anger is a very strange thing. At first, it's clear in your mind, exactly what you are angry about. But let that anger fester for a while and it morphs into a giant monster—filled with hatred that isn't about anything specific. Before long, the only thing you can remember is the anger. And that could leave you wondering why you liked this person in the first place.

When you're feeling frustrated and let down it is easy to sit around and wait for the other person to come up to you and suggest that you talk. After all, you are the injured party. Or at least that's how you see it. But it's possible that your friend is feeling the same way. And with both of you sitting in your rooms waiting for the phone to ring, no progress is going to be made. For the sake of your friendship, suck in your gut, bite the bullet, and be the bigger person. After a short cooling off period, suggest that you sit down and talk about things.

RULE 5
Learn to say "I am sorry".

They're only three little words. But "I am sorry" can be the hardest sentence you'll ever say. It's never easy to admit that you've made a mistake. But sometimes there's just no denying it. And when you're faced with the reality, the best thing to do is admit that you've done something you regret and ask for forgiveness.

RULE 6

To err is human, to forgive divine.

We've all heard that old saying, and basically it's true. Who do you know that hasn't made a mistake that has hurt someone else? There are no perfect people in this world. You just may be the very next one to make a big painful error. Wouldn't you want your friend to forgive you?

RULE 7

Sometimes the only thing to do is agree to disagree.

Once in a while, you and your friend will find yourselves going around in circles during an argument, with neither one of you willing to budge on your position. That's when you two have a big decision to make. Is this really worth risking your entire friendship over? Some things are. But most arguments are about the little things that don't mean much in the long run.

If you both have made an honest effort to understand each other's point of view, and you've made no headway, it may be time to agree to disagree. Lots of people have saved their relationships that way. Just look at James Carville and Mary Matalin. He was Bill Clinton's campaign adviser when Clinton ran for president against President George Bush. Mary Matalin was one of President Bush's campaign advisors in the same election. Talk about two people with plenty to argue about! But they agreed to disagree—and went on to get married!

Chapter Nine

Can You Keep a Secret?

Bet you can't count how many times the word *trust* is used in this book. That's because trust is one of the most important components in any friendship.

You can't keep it all inside!

There are all kinds of secrets. Some of them are wonderful—like the fact that the guy in English class who you've been staring at for weeks just told someone that he likes you, or finding out from your father's business associate that your favorite rock star is staying at a local hotel.

But other secrets are not so terrific. And holding in secrets that make you sad or angry can prove very stressful. After a while, the stress of hiding things will actually make you physically ill. Everybody needs somebody to spill their guts to once in a while.

If your friend entrusts you with a secret, most of the time it's up to you to keep the information just that— secret. You can't tell a soul that she's going to wind up taking Spanish in summer school if she doesn't pick up her grades soon, or that she has a big crush on the captain of the football team.

Keeping information that might embarrass your friend or hurt her feelings, is very important. If your friend knows she can trust you, she will feel free to tell you the things she needs to let out. And the two of you can work on finding a solution to her troubles without anybody else being the wiser.

But there's a big difference between a secret that

might embarrass your friend, and a secret that can cause her actual physical or mental harm.

Sometimes, secrets need to be told.

Part of trusting someone is knowing that she will always do what is in your best interest. And vice versa. If your friend tells you something in confidence, but you believe that she is in real danger, it is in your friend's best interest to reveal her secret to someone who can help her.

There's a big difference between the kind of harm most kids come up against in school—you know, being made fun of or being ostracized by some of their so-called friends—and real harm. If your friend

But I said I wouldn't tell...

tells you a secret that you think will make the other kids pick on her if you tell anyone, keep your mouth shut. But if your friend reveals to you that she may have an eating disorder or substance abuse problem, or that she has been threatened or abused, find an adult that you trust, and ask him or her to help your friend.

Even though you know you are doing the right thing by asking an adult for help with your friend's problem, don't expect your friend to come running to you with gratitude—at least not at first. She's more likely to be angry at you for revealing her secret. That's going to hurt, because you know that you only told someone in order to get your friend help. But hang tough, and know that you did the right thing, because the main thing is for your friend to get help with her problem, not for you to get gratitude or credit for helping her. And in the long run, she probably will come around and thank you for helping her out of a problem she just couldn't handle on her own.

And then your friendship will be stronger than ever.

Chapter Ten

What Would You Do?

Friendships obviously mean a lot to you. Otherwise, you wouldn't be reading this book right now. But how good of a friend are you? If you want to find out, answer the questions below. Then check the answers section at the end of this quiz to find out what you can do to become an even better friend than you already are.

1. You and your best friend are trying on clothes in the mall. She puts on a sweater that looks awful on her. What do you do?

    A. Tell her the truth—it's better that she hear it from you now than if she buys it and wears it to school.

    B. Make her feel good by telling her how wonderful she looks.

C. Suggest that she might look better in a different color or style, and volunteer to go out on the floor and find something for her.

So... Is this me? Or what?

2. Your friend is throwing a big party. Her invitation list includes two girls who are considered total geeks by everyone else in your crowd. What do you do?

    A. You don't say a word and let your friend invite who she likes, even though you are really worried that all of your other friends won't attend.

    B. In order to avoid attending a party with geeks, you politely bow out, telling your friend you have a family function to attend.

C. Tell your friend how you feel, but go to the party, anyway.

3. Your friend just tried out for the school musical—and didn't get the part. You figured that might happen, since your friend doesn't sing as well as she thinks she does. What do you tell her?

   A. "They made a mistake—you were terrific at your audition!"

   B. "Be happy you didn't make it. That play is going to stink!"

   C. "I'm sorry you didn't make it. Hey, do you want to work on the costumes committee with me?"

4. You get a bigger allowance than your friend. You know she really wants a new CD by her favorite group, but she says she doesn't have the cash. Do you...

   A. Offer to loan her the money.

   B. Keep your own spending down so she doesn't feel bad.

   C. Convince her that it's worth being broke if she'll really enjoys the CD.

5. You are invited to a party and your best friend isn't. She feels really bad about not being invited, and calls you up. "Were you invited?" she asks. What do you do?

  A. Don't tell your friend that you were invited to the party, but go anyway.

  B. Admit to her that you were invited. Then go to the party, and make a silent promise not to bring it up to her.

  C. Refuse to go to the party unless your friend is invited.

6. Your friend has already borrowed—and ruined—two of your favorite shirts. Now she's returning your new jacket with a soda stain on it. Do you...

  A. Keep your mouth shut and take the jacket to the cleaners.

  B. Decide never to loan her another thing.

  C. Ask her to have the jacket laundered.

7. Your friend is absolutely obsessed with a new pop group. She is constantly telling you all about who the group members are dating, and what their favorite colors are. The next time she pulls out an article about them do you...

A. Listen as she reads and try to act interested.

B. Tell her honestly that you really don't care about the group.

C. Pretend to listen but think about something else.

8. You overhear an unflattering rumor about your friend. Do you:

A. Rush over and tell her what you heard, before she hears it from someone who doesn't care about her as much as you do.

B. Interrupt the conversation and defend your friend.

C. Ignore the rumor and assume people will know it's a lie.

9. You and your best friend have plans for Saturday night. Suddenly the cutest guy in the school—the one your best friend knows you've been drooling over for six months—asks you to the movies. What do you do?

A. Tell your best friend what happened, and hope she'll understand that you just have to say yes to him.

B. Tell the guy you're sorry, but you have plans.

C. Cancel on your friend and say yes. You owe it to yourself.

10. You meet a new girl at school who is your total soul mate. You like the same music, you wear the same kinds of clothes, you even cry at the same movies. There's just one problem. Your best friend can't stand your new friend. What do you do?

A. Decide to choose one friend and drop the other.

B. Force your two new friends to get together with you as often as possible. It's a little tense but at least you get to see both of them.

C. Hang out with both girls, but separately.

Here's What You Should Do:

1. The best solution to this dilemma would be **C**. Telling someone they look awful isn't very nice, especially if you're not offering any solutions to the problem. And lying shouldn't be part of any true friendship. By offering to find something more flattering for your friend to wear, you are helping her to better herself.

2. The best answer here is **A**. It's not your party, so the guest list is not up to you. No matter who her other friends are, you owe it to your friend to be there for her big night. Chances are she already knows how the other people in your crowd feel. She just doesn't care what they think. Maybe you shouldn't either.

3. It's obvious your friend wanted to be in the play. But telling her that she was wonderful when she wasn't, isn't really fair to her, or to the show's director. And telling her that the show isn't going to be any good won't make her feel better either. Perhaps the best thing to do would be to join her backstage doing costumes, makeup, publicity, or scenery, answer **C**. You can be together, you can be part of the show, and you might even meet some new friends.

4. The nicest choice here would be **B**. Although your intentions might be the best, offering to loan her the cash may make it appear that you are flaunting your money. And convincing her to buy the CD isn't really fair to her either—you don't know what's in her bank account. Keeping your spending down will keep your friend from feeling embarrassed about her financial situation, and it won't hurt you either.

5. Believe it or not, the true friend answer here is **B**. Obviously, lying about the invitation is a total no—friends don't lie. But not going to the party isn't fair to you—you and your friend should meet and befriend other people. There's no reason you shouldn't go to the party, but reminding her of that would be unfair. So go, enjoy yourself, and make sure to do something special with your friend the very next day.

6. It's your friend's responsibility to make sure that what she borrows comes back in good condition.

She needs to learn a little responsibility—and she won't if you keep cleaning up after her. By asking her to clean your jacket, answer **C**, she'll get the message, and hopefully learn her lesson.

7. A good friend would do as it says in answer **A**. It's nice to take an interest in what your friends like. Besides, you don't know which of your hobbies she finds boring. Wouldn't you want her to give you the same respect?

8. Defending your friend, answer **B**, is the way to go. Telling her about the rumor will only hurt her feelings and she'll probably feel pretty helpless. And ignoring it won't help her either. You never know what people will believe. If a rumor hangs around in the air long enough, folks often perceive it as the truth.

9. Sorry, but you really should turn down Mr. Dream Date, answer **B**. Guilting your friend into telling you it's okay for you to break your plans with her, isn't fair. And simply canceling with her sends the message that she's not very important in your life. Boyfriends may come and go, but true friends stick around. There's no sense in risking your friendship. Besides, by turning him down (and suggesting a rain date), you'll give yourself an air of mystery that he'll find hard to resist!

10. Your answer here is clearly **C**. You shouldn't have to choose between friends (and anyone who asks you to do that is not a real friend!). Getting your two friends together a few times to see if they can work things out is a great idea. But after a while, if it still isn't working, you'll have to accept that they won't ever see eye to eye. Try hanging out with each girl separately. But should you decide to have a party or something, don't feel you have to invite only one girl. Every now and then your two buddies will have to be civil to each other, for your sake.

romantic towards him? Or are you so anxious to have a boyfriend that you are convincing yourself it just might work? Have your friends influenced your feelings by telling you how obvious it is that the two of you belong together? Is this just a passing feeling, or the real deal? You need to sort out your emotions before you open up the conversation with your best friend, because once you take your relationship down this new path, the rules change.

Many people believe that the best romantic relationships begin as friendships, mostly because both people know so much about each other. But another fact

Chapter Eleven

Under One Roof

Your little brother read your diary—and told everyone what was inside. Your older sister insists on
playing depressing music all day long—even though

Ahgrrr!
Stop it!

MY DIARY

you constantly remind her that it's your room, too, and you'd like to hear one of your CDs for a change. Your mother keeps telling you that you have to do your laundry before you go to the mall, and your dad just wants everybody to be quiet for fifteen minutes so he can read the paper.

All of which leads you to wonder, "How could these people possibly be my family, let alone my friends?"

Turning your family into friends may seem nearly impossible, but it isn't. Even though your household may sometimes seem more like a war zone than home sweet home, making friends with your family is a good idea. Maybe an idea you never even thought of.

As long as you are in school, chances are you are going to spend more time with the people in your house than with anybody else. So doesn't it make sense to try and keep the peace once in a while?

The best way to do that is treat your family with the same patience and respect you give to your friends. Sounds impossible, huh? Relax, *The Friendship Hotline* is here to help!

My little brother is making me CRAZY!!

Imagine a brother and sister who really get along. They don't compete for attention, they never tease each other, they never get angry at each other. Do you have a good picture in your imagination of this delightful duo? Good. Because that's the only place a relationship like that will ever exist.

According to the experts, there's always sibling rivalry, except in a family with just one child! Brothers and sisters naturally compete, mostly in an unconscious desire for their parents' attention and approval. So you can forget about that ideal brother and sister relationship. It's not going to happen.

Of course that doesn't mean that you and your sibs can't get along most of the time. Having a brother or a sister isn't a curse. It can actually be a gift. Nobody will ever understand you quite the way your siblings will. They've shared your childhood. And that means you will always have more in common with them than you will with almost anybody else.

The trick to being friendly with your brothers and sisters is to think of them as friends instead of relatives. Try and figure out why they behave the way they do, and then do what you can to remain on good terms with them.

Say your little brother has been peeking in your diary, listening in on your phone calls, and hanging around when you have friends over. That kind of behavior just makes you want to scream, doesn't it? But before you open your mouth and break the sound barrier, take a moment to think about what your little brother is really telling you. It sounds like he just wants a little attention from you. Look at it from his point of view. You're getting older, and you're changing. Suddenly you're more private. You have friends and secrets and a whole life that he's not part of. And while that may be the most normal thing in the world, it can hurt your younger brother's feelings. (Of course he's going to be the same way in a couple of years, but he doesn't realize that yet.)

So, instead of reading your little brother the riot act, why not read him a book? Or ask him if he wants to go out and have a catch. All he wants is to be a part of your life. If you give him that, the snooping will probably come to an end.

And what about that older sister of yours? Maybe her moody music is getting you down. But think about how you would react if one of your friends seemed sad and always walked around with depressing songs on her Walkman. What would you do? Well, being the terrific friend that you are, you'd probably ask her if anything was wrong, and offer her a shoulder to cry on if she needed it. Try doing the same thing with your

older sister. Even if she's not sure she wants to share her troubles with you, she'll appreciate the effort, and that will bring the two of you closer than ever.

It's not their fault.

Sometimes you can find yourself getting angry at your brothers and sisters for something they didn't even do. Every now and then, parents, teachers, and even some of your friends will compare you to your sibs. When they tell you that you are more helpful, studious, or fun than your sibs, that kind of comparison is easy to take (although, think about how it must make your sibs feel!). But when the tables are turned and your brother or sister comes out smelling like a rose, the comparisons can really sting. And often, instead of getting mad at the person who is making the comparison, you get mad at your brother or sister.

That's when you have to take a moment to cool down and think. There's no reason for you to resent your brother or sister. He or she is not at fault here. The person you are angry with is the one who made the comparison. You need to focus your attention on the person who has really hurt your feelings.

You do need to tell your mother, father, teacher, or friend how you feel. Whether or not what you say will get you any results all depends on the words you choose and the tone of voice you use to say them. You have to remember that screaming, yelling, or crying never helps any volatile situation. In the end throwing a major fit will only make things worse.

Instead, take a deep breath and use your calmest voice to politely say something like, "I'm not my brother or my sister. I have my strengths and weaknesses, just like they do. I would appreciate it if you would not compare me to anybody else."

No one can get mad at you for that. Chances are your mom, dad, teacher, or friend never even realized how they were hurting your feelings by making comparisons between you and your siblings. By pointing it out to them, the comparisons may very well stop. And that's good for you and your brothers and sisters.

I'm not my brother or my sister....

My buddies: Mom and Dad!

Turning parents into friends may seem nearly impossible. After all, your parents control the cash flow, and they make the rules. Automatically, that puts them in a position of power. And technically, no one should be in control in a friendship.

But you do actually have some control over the way you and your parents get along. Parent/child relationships are often filled with petty arguments over silly things like how loud the music is, or how long a telephone conversation needs to be. The trick to keeping those arguments to a minimum is to treat them the same way you treat your arguments with your friends. The same rules apply—give yourself time to cool down, and try to reach a compromise that makes everyone happy.

You might also try anticipating what will make your parents upset. If you know your dad wants you to get your homework done before you watch TV, but there's a soap opera you just have to watch, let modern technology help you keep the peace. Pop a tape in the VCR when you get home. Then go up to your room right away and get started on that geography.

If your mom sounds especially tired when she calls you from the office, you can probably figure that she's going to be in no mood to clean the family room when she gets home. Why not do her a favor and straighten it up? You might even try your hand at cooking dinner, too (if you're allowed to use the stove and oven when nobody's home). Remember: A grateful mom is a happy mom. And happy moms are less likely to get angry.

If this all sounds like you are doing all the work and your parents are reaping all the benefits, remember that the goal here is compromise.   By doing your homework and helping out around the house, you are demonstrating your maturity. When your parents see what a responsible kid you are, they are likely to give you more privileges. And that way everybody wins!

Chapter Twelve

It's Hard to Say Good-bye

One of the problems with being a kid is that so many things are out of your control. There you are, happy with your school, happy with your team, happy with your friends, and your parents lower the boom. YOUR FAMILY IS MOVING!

Life is full of changes. And change can be hard—especially on friendships. Your first thought is bound to be that you'll be forgotten by your friends. You know, out of sight, out of mind.

But it doesn't have to be that way. There's another expression—absence makes the heart grow fonder. Which way will your friendship go? That all depends on the kind of people you and your best friend are.

Some people have no problems saying good-bye to their friends. They live totally in the present. Whomever they are near is their friend. Other people like to hold on to the past. They see friendship as a lifelong commitment—a string that binds two people no matter where they may wander.

You may not know which kind of person you are, or which kind of person your friend is until you are faced with one of you moving away. If you are both the same type of person, this new transition will cause you little trouble. But if one of you tends to live in the moment, and the other tends to hold on to the past, you're both going to wind up feeling hurt. The friend who doesn't see friendship as a lifelong relationship will feel guilty when faced with her friend's need to keep the friendship alive. The friend who is trying to hang on will feel abandoned.

There's no real answer to this problem. The truth is, life's changes will affect your friendships. If you try and convince yourself that nothing will change, you're only lying to yourself. And because you are your own best friend, you have a responsibility to face the truth. Once you've accepted that truth you can work with your friend to find ways to make the changes less painful.

D-liver D-letter D-sooner D-better!

No doubt about it, keeping your long distance friendship alive is going to take equal effort on the part of both friends. But if you both wish to remain close, it's not impossible. Here are a few suggestions.

1. **_Write letters._** An obvious suggestion, but one worth stating. There's nothing more exciting than getting something in the mail. Be sure to include photos in your letters so you can keep up with each other's new hairstyles and clothing. Letters on tape are really fun, especially when you include snippets of your favorite new songs on them. If you are feeling extremely ambitious, ask to borrow your parents' video camera, and mail your friend a video tour of your new home or her old neighborhood.

2. **_Phone her._** Another no-brainer suggestion! They say the telephone is the next best thing to being there, and the truth is, nothing can pick you up faster than hearing your best friend's voice. But

phone calls can be expensive, so you may want to keep the calls short, and trade off on which friend does the calling.

3. **Dash off a quick E-mail.** E-mail is the easiest way in the world to stay in touch. As long as you're researching that history report on the Net, why not take a break and send your friend a quick note. E-mail has the advantage of being very immediate, and easy to send. It's also a lot cheaper than those long-distance phone calls. But because you don't know if other members of your friend's family have access to her E-mail addie, save the intimate details for the regular mail.

4. **Make vacation plans.** Ask your parents if you and your best friend can get together over vacations. Maybe she can come to your new house for the winter break, or you might be able to return to the old neighborhood in the spring. When summer comes, try to arrange to go to the same summer camp. That way you'll be able to spend weeks together!

I've tried everything, but I still feel the friendship slipping away.

Even with all of these tips, there's still the possibility that your friendship will not withstand the changes of a move. And when that happens, you have to be ready to let the friendship go.

Although it is painful to watch a friendship silently slip through your fingers, sometimes it's the best thing for everyone involved. Remember that no experience in life is a total loss. You learn from everything. You will bring the experiences you shared with your friend to your next relationship.

And don't give up your hope of someday rekindling your friendship.

Chapter Thirteen

Details, Details!

From the outside, some friendships seem to be touched by magic. It seems as though they are effortless relationships that flow as naturally as a river.

But don't kid yourself. No relationship is that smooth. (Even rivers have rocky bottoms and rapids

running through them!) All friendships require hard work to keep them going. Some are more difficult than others, but often the ones that are the toughest to maintain are the ones that are the most worth keeping.

Little things mean a lot to a friend—like remembering what her zodiac sign is (so you can send her horoscope to her from the newspaper while she's away at summer camp) or remembering what her favorite color is (for when you are searching for that perfect holiday gift).

To keep track of the details, fill in this address list, and check it every once in a while:

January

Name
_____

Address
_____

_____

Phone
_____

E-mail
_____

Birthday
_____

Zodiac Sign
_____

Favorite Color
_____

Name

Address

Phone

E-mail

Birthday

Zodiac Sign

Favorite Color

February

Name

Address

Phone

E-mail

Birthday

Zodiac Sign

Favorite Color

Name
_____

Address
_____

_____

Phone
_____

E-mail
_____

Birthday
_____

Zodiac Sign
_____

Favorite Color
_____

March

Name
_____

Address
_____

_____

Phone
_____

E-mail
_____

Birthday
_____

Zodiac Sign
_____

Favorite Color
_____

Name _____

Address _____

_____

Phone _____

E-mail _____

Birthday _____

Zodiac Sign _____

Favorite Color _____

April

Name _____

Address _____

_____

Phone _____

E-mail _____

Birthday _____

Zodiac Sign _____

Favorite Color _____

Name
_____

Address
_____

_____

Phone
_____

E-mail
_____

Birthday
_____

Zodiac Sign
_____

Favorite Color
_____

May

Name
_____

Address
_____

_____

Phone
_____

E-mail
_____

Birthday
_____

Zodiac Sign
_____

Favorite Color
_____

Name

Address

Phone

E-mail

Birthday

Zodiac Sign

Favorite Color

June

Name

Address

Phone

E-mail

Birthday

Zodiac Sign

Favorite Color

Name
_____

Address
_____

_____

Phone
_____

E-mail
_____

Birthday
_____

Zodiac Sign
_____

Favorite Color
_____

July

Name
_____

Address
_____

_____

Phone
_____

E-mail
_____

Birthday
_____

Zodiac Sign
_____

Favorite Color
_____

Name

Address

Phone

E-mail

Birthday

Zodiac Sign

Favorite Color

August

Name

Address

Phone

E-mail

Birthday

Zodiac Sign

Favorite Color

Name _____

Address _____

_____

Phone _____

E-mail _____

Birthday _____

Zodiac Sign _____

Favorite Color _____

September

Name _____

Address _____

_____

Phone _____

E-mail _____

Birthday _____

Zodiac Sign _____

Favorite Color _____

Name

Address

Phone

E-mail

Birthday

Zodiac Sign

Favorite Color

October

Name

Address

Phone

E-mail

Birthday

Zodiac Sign

Favorite Color

Name _____

Address _____

_____

Phone _____

E-mail _____

Birthday _____

Zodiac Sign _____

Favorite Color _____

November

Name _____

Address _____

_____

Phone _____

E-mail _____

Birthday _____

Zodiac Sign _____

Favorite Color _____

Name

Address

Phone

E-mail

Birthday

Zodiac Sign

Favorite Color

December

Name

Address

Phone

E-mail

Birthday

Zodiac Sign

Favorite Color

Name

Address

Phone

E-mail

Birthday

Zodiac Sign

Favorite Color

Chapter Fourteen

Do You Want to Chat?

Imagine having friends in Rome, London, Paris, and New York. Well, you don't have to be a jet-setter to talk to people all over the world. You just have to have a computer.

Did you know that?

Well that's not what I heard!

The World Wide Web has allowed people from different cultures to meet, chat, and become friendly. It's an amazing invention that has opened our minds, and expanded our abilities to form friendships.

But while there are an infinite number of benefits to being hooked up to the Internet, there are dangers lurking beyond your keyboard. But that doesn't mean you should unplug your modem. You just have to play it smart and steer away from trouble while you're driving on the information superhighway.

Welcome to the chat room.

Feel like talking to someone about how awful that last episode of your favorite sitcom was? Do you want to know if anyone else out there has heard the new single from your favorite group—and liked it as much as you do? Are you looking for advice from some other kid who has problems with a bully in school?

Search the Internet long enough and you can find kids willing to discuss almost any topic. There are literally thousands of chat rooms on the Net, where you can talk to other people about the things that interest you.

Chat rooms can be a lot of fun. There's something very exciting about communicating with people who don't know anything about you. Sometimes even major celebrities can be found chatting away with their fans, whether on Web sites developed by magazines like *Teen People*, or anonymously in chat rooms (Leonardo Di Caprio has often said that he surfs the Net anonymously to see what people are saying about him!).

Many people feel very free and open on the Internet. The insecurities that might cause them to become shy in real life (like their weight, their height, their grades, or even the kind of house they live in) are not an issue on the Net. Nobody can see you in cyberspace. And nobody knows your past. The only information people on the Net have about you are the words you type into your computer. That's why many people who have difficulties making friends at school, have no problem becoming friendly with people in cyberspace. When they are online, they feel more free to speak their minds about their favorite topics.

Beware of ghosts!

But the very thing that makes the Internet such a wonderful place, is the same thing that makes it so dangerous. Because no one can see or hear the voices of anyone on the Internet, it is easy for people to pretend to be what they are not.

People who pretend to be someone they're not are called *ghosts*. Ghosts aren't necessarily bad people,

sometimes they are just girls or guys who are living out their fantasies—like telling other people online that they are captain of their cheerleading squad or president of the student council.

There's really no harm in telling little white lies like that on the Net. But some ghosts are dangerous. Usually they are adults who pose as teens and join in on teenager-oriented chat rooms. These adults are often up to no good.

But there are ways to protect yourself from ghosts who mean you harm. For starters, never use your real name on the Internet. When you enter a chat room, make up a name. And no matter what, don't give out your home address, telephone number, age, or the city you live in. There's no reason that anyone online has to know those things, and that kind of information can make you easy to trace—something you want to avoid at all costs. If anyone on line asks you for your phone number or address, check out of the chat room immediately, and tell an adult what happened.

Some Internet servers will offer to set up a personality profile for you. A profile is supposed to be used by online advertisers who want to send you information on products they think people in your region or age range might be interested in. But profiles can also be accessed and used by people who are less interested in targeting products toward kids than they are in causing trouble for kids.

It's probably safest to skip the whole profile thing. But if you really do want to have a profile online, first check with your parents. Then make sure you don't give out any personal information — including your real name and your age. If you want advertisers to know what region you live in, give the state and the country. Don't list the city. And while it's okay to state some of your hobbies or interests, stay away from any information that might reveal your age or sex, like your favorite TV shows or music groups.

Tom Hanks looked so cute when he finally met Meg Ryan in the park at the end of You've Got Mail.

No doubt about it. That final scene of *You've Got Mail*, when Meg Ryan (code name "Shop girl") met her cyberspace confidante in the park was really romantic. Imagine, two chat room buddies meeting and falling in love. It does happen—there are articles about couples who met on the Internet in all the major magazines.

But remember, Meg and Tom (and the other folks

who have met friends and lovers on the Net) are adults. As a kid, you are more susceptible to being harmed by someone who isn't really who he or she claims to be. So here's a cyberspace rule you shouldn't break, no matter what! DO NOT MEET SOMEONE IN PERSON WHOM YOU MET ON THE INTERNET!!

If someone you've been chatting with suggests that you meet, turn that person down flat and move on to another chat room.

Can I give out my E-mail address?

Suppose you meet someone in a chat room, and the two of you really hit it off. Is it okay to give that person your E-mail address?

It's safest not to give out your E-mail address to people you don't know, because it is very easy to track someone down via their E-mail address. It's better to arrange to meet again in a chat room at a specific time and date. Some Internet carriers also have buddy systems, in which two people who are both customers of the same Internet carrier can arrange to chat with one another without interruptions from other people. Before you sign on to one of the buddy systems however, first check with your parents. Then contact your Internet carrier to find out what precautions are in place to make sure that your identity is kept secret.

Don't let all of these precautions frighten you away from surfing the Net, and talking with other teens in chat rooms. You can learn a lot, and you can meet some interesting new people. (Although it is difficult to establish the intimacy of a true friendship on the Net.) The Net is just like anything else—it can be great, as long as you play by the rules.

Chapter Fifteen

The Last Word

Friends turn up in all sorts of places. You can find them in school, in clubs, online, or just walking down the street. That's why it's so important to keep your heart and mind open to the idea of meeting new people from all walks of life. Don't count someone out because

of what she wears or who she knows or where she hangs out. You have to give her a chance. After all, you never know who will turn out to be your closest friend.

Your friendships are the most important relationships you'll have. So treat them as you would a valuable gift: Be grateful for your friendships. Find ways to keep them fresh and exciting. And take the time to fix things in your relationships when something has gone wrong.

Remember that you can only gain from a friendship if you put effort into it. As you help your friends learn, grow, and feel good about themselves, you will learn, grow, and develop a great self-image that will help you in everything you do.

Elizabeth Barrett Browning was a poet who knew what real friendships were about. This poem just about says it all.

> *I love you not only for what you are,*
> *but for what I am when I am with you.*
> *I love you not only for what you have*
>   *made of yourself,*
> *but for what you have made of me*
> *I love you for the part of me that you*
>   *bring out.*
>
> —*Elizabeth Barrett Browning*